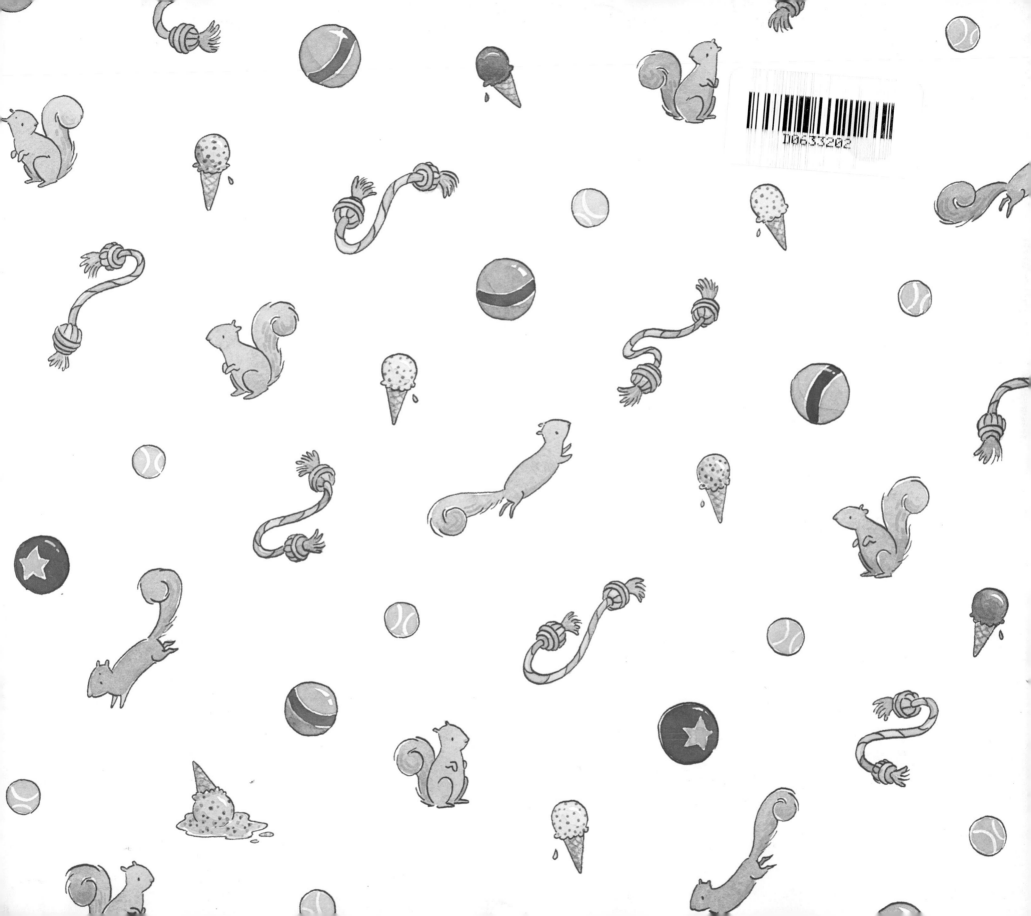

written by Trudy Krisher   illustrated by Brooke Boynton-Hughes

Bark Park!

Beach Lane Books · New York London Toronto Sydney New Delhi

Paws pat the door.
Tails thump the floor.

Dogs sit and wait.

Dogs through the gate.

Dogs at the park. . . .

Bark! Bark! Bark!

Dog in a hat.

Dog on a lap.

Dogs on a ride.

Dogs down a slide.

Dogs chewing bones.

Dogs licking cones.

Dogs in the sun.

Dogs on the run.

Dogs with a buddy.

Dogs getting muddy.

Dogs at the park. . . .

Bark!

Dogs have explored.

Dogs are adored.

Dogs take a drink.

Dogs yawn and blink.

Dogs in a heap.

Dogs go to sleep . . .

and dream in the dark . . .

Park! Park! Park!

Arfs, woofs, and yips to Buddy, Buffy,
Carmela, Molly, Oscar, Riley, and Spenser—T. K.

For Kate, Liam, and Ryan.
And for Domino, the first dog I ever loved—B. B.-H.

BEACH LANE BOOKS • An imprint of Simon & Schuster Children's Publishing Division • 1230 Avenue of the Americas, New York, New York 10020 • Text copyright © 2018 by Trudy Krisher • Illustrations copyright © 2018 by Brooke Boynton-Hughes • All rights reserved, including the right of reproduction in whole or in part in any form. • BEACH LANE BOOKS is a trademark of Simon & Schuster, Inc. • For information about special discounts for bulk purchases, please contact Simon & Schuster Special Sales at 1-866-506-1949 or business@simonandschuster.com. • The Simon & Schuster Speakers Bureau can bring authors to your live event. For more information or to book an event, contact the Simon & Schuster Speakers Bureau at 1-866-248-3049 or visit our website at www.simonspeakers.com. • Book design by Lauren Rille • The text for this book was set in Supernett. • The illustrations for this book were rendered in pen & ink, watercolor, and colored pencil. • Manufactured in China • 0118 SCP • First Edition • 10 9 8 7 6 5 4 3 2 1 • Library of Congress Cataloging-in-Publication Data • Names: Krisher, Trudy, author. | Boynton-Hughes, Brooke, illustrator. • Title: Bark Park / Trudy Krisher ; illustrated by Brooke Boynton-Hughes. • Description: First edition. | New York : Beach Lane Books, [2018] | Summary: Told in rhyming text, dogs have a wonderful day at the dog park. • Identifiers: LCCN 2017014898 | ISBN 9781481430753 (hardcover : alk. paper) | ISBN 9781481430760 (eBook) • Subjects: | CYAC: Stories in rhyme. | Dogs—Fiction. | Classification: LCC PZ8.3.K89 Bar 2018 | DDC [E]—dc23 LC record available at https://lccn.loc.gov/2017014898

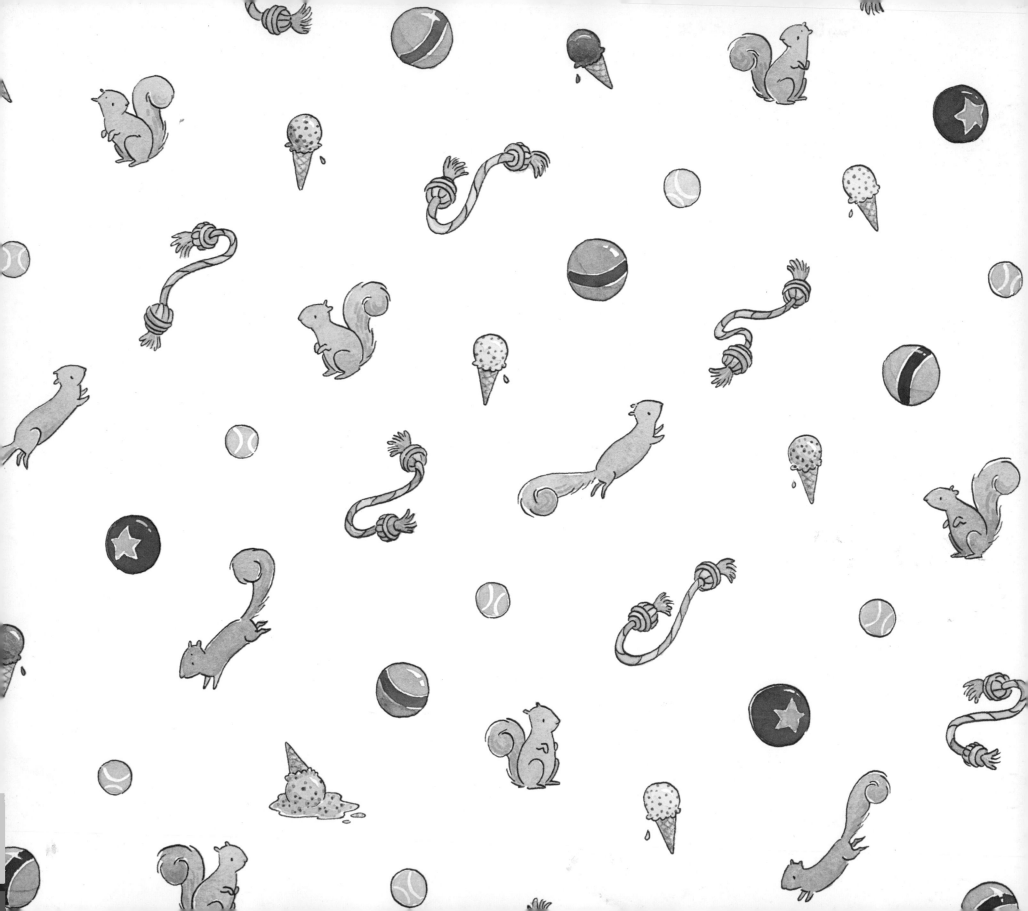